Abigail picked up her pen. "*When I grow up,* she wrote, "*I mean to be a witch. Because there's no other way to deal with some people. It'd be fun . . .*" She sucked her pen a bit and added, "*. . . to turn some people into frogs.*"

As far as Abigail knew, she had never met anyone who could turn a person into a frog. Nor any frogs who had been turned. All the same, she said to herself, there are *some* people who definitely need it!

YOUNG CORGI BOOKS

Young Corgi books are perfect when you are looking for great books to read on your own. They are full of exciting stories and entertaining pictures and can be tackled with confidence. There are funny books, scary books, spine-tingling stories and mysterious ones. Whatever your interests you'll find something in Young Corgi to suit you: from ponies to football, from families to ghosts. The books are written by some of the most famous and popular of today's children's authors, and by some of the best new talents, too.

Whether you read one chapter a night, or devour the whole book in one sitting, you'll love Young Corgi Books. The more you read, the more you'll want to read! Why not try:

ANIMAL CRACKERS by Narinder Dhami
ASTRID, THE AU PAIR FROM
OUTER SPACE by Emily Smith
BLACK QUEEN by Michael Morpurgo
THE DAD LIBRARY by Dennis Whelehan
SAMMY'S SUPER SEASON
by Lindsay Camp

A Witch in the Classroom!

Ghillian Potts

Illustrated by Jan Lewis

A WITCH IN THE CLASSROOM!
A YOUNG CORGI BOOK : 0 552 54685 2

First published in Great Britain by Young Corgi Books

PRINTING HISTORY
Young Corgi edition published 2000

5 7 9 10 8 6 4

Set in 16/20 pt Bembo Schoolbook by
Phoenix Typesetting, Ilkley, West Yorkshire.

Young Corgi Books are published by Transworld Publishers,
61–63 Uxbridge Road, London W5 5SA,
a division of The Random House Group Ltd,
in Australia by Random House Australia (Pty) Ltd,
20 Alfred Street, Milsons Points, Sydney, NSW 2061, Australia,
in New Zealand by Random House New Zealand Ltd,
18 Poland Road, Glenfield, Auckland 10, New Zealand
and in South Africa by Random House (Pty) Ltd,
Endulini, 5a Jubilee Road, Parktown 2193, South Africa.

Printed and bound in Great Britain by
Cox & Wyman Ltd, Reading, Berkshire.

*Dedicated to
the children of
the Gordon School, Eltham,
who contributed so much to the story*

Contents

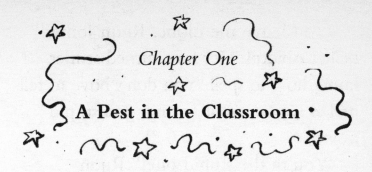

Chapter One

A Pest in the Classroom

"All right, children! Quiet, everybody,"
called Mrs Treasure. She pushed a
dangling hairpin back into her
straggling hair and clapped her hands.
"Excuse me! *Excuse me!*"

No-one listened. Abigail and Ryan
were having another set-to.

"You leave me alone, Ryan James!" yelled Abigail. Her face turned scarlet. "I know how to spell. You don't have to tell me! *And* you got it wrong, you stupid nowt!"

"You're the stupid one!" Ryan sneered. "Can't even talk proper. I don't believe there's such a word as 'nowt'." And he snapped his fingers under Abigail's nose.

That did it. Abigail went from scarlet to crimson. She couldn't snap her fingers, no matter how hard she tried. It made her absolutely furious when someone did it to her. She lunged forward, mouth wide, and did her best to bite Ryan's fingers.

"Abigail! Abigail Pengelly! What do you think you are doing?" Mrs Treasure grabbed Abigail's arm and hauled her away from Ryan. 'Go and sit down at your table!" she ordered. "You too, Ryan. I don't want a squeak out of either of you till dinner time. Now, simmer down, everyone, please."

Ryan glared at Abigail and Abigail glared at Ryan. Mrs Treasure turned to help Michael with his work. Ryan at once reached over and stabbed Abigail in the arm with his specially sharpened pencil. Mrs Treasure didn't notice. She was leaning over Michael.

I wish, I *wish* there was some way to make Mrs Treasure notice Ryan when he's being horrible to me! thought Abigail.

Ryan made a rude noise. Several people looked round. Ryan held his nose and looked accusingly at Abigail.

Abigail nearly burst with rage. There was no way she could get back at Ryan for that. Anything she said or did would make things worse. Already she could see Sophie sniggering. She'd be getting ready to whisper the news to everyone she could.

Abigail picked up her workbook and pen and walked right out of the room.

"Miss!" shouted several voices. "Miss! Abigail's gone!"

Mrs Treasure came after her. She looked flustered and worried. "Abigail, whatever is wrong with you today?" she asked.

"There's nothing wrong with *me*," Abigail told her. "It's that – that slimy toad, Ryan James! I'm not sitting next to him any longer! Not one more minute. Or I'll run away. I'll – I'll kill him! I'll fill his pants with itching powder!"

"You've made your point," said Mrs

Treasure. She smiled at Abigail. "I'll deal with Ryan."

They went back into the classroom.

Mrs Treasure cleared her throat loudly. "Sophie, sit down, please. Ryan, I want you to go and sit at . . . Let me see . . ."

Ryan grinned and got up.

"Oh, please, miss, let him sit by me again!" begged Sophie. She gazed up, her eyes wide.

"Certainly not!" Mrs Treasure looked around the room. "Pat, change places with Ryan, please."

Pat was furious. She stomped over to Abigail's table and slumped down on the empty chair. "It's your fault," she told Abigail. "I don't want to sit here. I want to be with my friends." She turned her back and began to work with loud sighs and groans.

Abigail shrugged. At least Ryan wasn't near her.

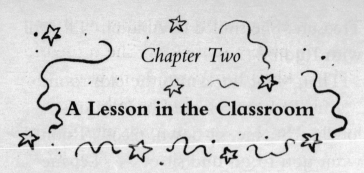

Chapter Two

A Lesson in the Classroom

But after dinner Ryan was back. Mrs Treasure didn't seem to care. Abigail watched him warily. Only yesterday he'd pulled her chair away as she was about to sit down. She still hurt from it.

"Now we're going to do some writing," said Mrs Treasure cheerfully.

"Let's see if you all remember how to make a proper sentence." She turned to the blackboard and began to write.

"*When I grow up, I mean to be . . .*" wrote Mrs Treasure in large pink letters.

"Oh, not again!" groaned Abigail. "We did this last week!"

"This time, I want you all to finish this sentence and then write two more, explaining why," said Mrs Treasure. She looked round the room. "Abigail, I hope you are listening."

"Yes, miss," said Abigail. Out of the corner of her eye she could see Ryan grinning. He held up his vicious pencil and pretended to jab her. Abigail showed her teeth at him.

"I want just three sentences, no more, no less," said Mrs Treasure. "Proper ones, with a capital letter at the beginning and a full stop at the end. All right, everyone? Away you go!"

Abigail looked sideways at Ryan. He was already writing and she could guess what it was. He always said he would be a businessman and make lots of money and buy a big house and, and, and . . . At least while he was writing he wasn't tying her shoelaces together.

Abigail picked up her pen. "*When I grow up,*" she wrote, "*I mean to be a witch. Because there's no other way to deal with some people. It'd be fun . . .*" She sucked her pen a bit and added, ". . . *to turn some people into frogs.*"

As far as Abigail knew, she had never met anyone who could turn a person into a frog. Nor any frogs who had been turned. All the same, she said to herself, there are *some* people who definitely need it!

Ryan was still writing. Abigail thought what an ugly boy he was. Nasty, too. But he'd make a handsome frog. She began to think of a spell to turn him into one. *"Ryan James ought to be a frog. He belongs in a bog,"* she began.

Then they had to hand in their writing.

Abigail was surprised when Mrs Treasure gave back their work. She didn't say a word about witches. "Abigail, you have not written three sentences," was all she said.

"But I did!" said Abigail. "I put a capital at the beginning and a stop at the end, just the way you said!"

"You can't start a sentence with

17

'Because','" Mrs Treasure explained. "Write it out properly, with a third sentence. Now, please."

So Abigail sucked her pen and scowled and wrote. "*When I grow up, I mean to be a witch because there's no other way to deal with some people. It'd be fun to turn some people into frogs. Most witches have animals called Familiars to help them.*"

"Thank you, Abigail," said Mrs Treasure. "You may go."

At the door Abigail looked back. Mrs Treasure was reading Abigail's work and smiling.

Chapter Three

A Rat in the Bedroom

Abigail walked home and went straight up to her bedroom. She wanted to feed and play with her pet rat, Gnasher. Gnasher's front half was dark brown but her back half was white. She looked as if she had been dipped in whitewash. Some people thought she looked funny. Abigail didn't.

Gnasher did not live up to her name. She'd never bitten anyone. Now and then she got excited but when that happened she just ran into the exercise wheel and whizzed it around.

As usual, Abigail told her about her day. Gnasher listened and twitched her whiskers. The whiskers tickled Abigail's fingers and sometimes Gnasher licked Abigail in a friendly way. Abigail felt better.

She put her hand into the cage and Gnasher stepped carefully onto her palm. Abigail lifted the rat out and put

her on her shoulder. She'd nicked some grapes from the kitchen. She gave Gnasher one to nibble and began to eat the rest of the handful herself.

"I wish I could be a witch," she told the rat. "I'm tired of that Ryan playing nasty tricks and sticking his pencil into me. Do you know, he sharpens it specially, every day! If I was a witch, I'd break the point in the machine each time he tried to sharpen it." She sighed. "I wonder how you learn magic. I do wish I could learn on my own."

She thought about it. "Do you know, Gnasher, I think perhaps I'll try! After all, I almost made a spell today to turn that nasty creep Ryan into a frog. First, I suppose, I ought to have a Familiar. Would you like to be my Familiar, Gnasher?"

"I thought you'd never ask," said the rat.

Chapter Four

A Toad in the Park

Abigail choked on the last grape. She coughed so hard that Gnasher almost fell off her shoulder. The rat dug her sharp little claws into Abigail's collar and squeaked crossly in her ear.

"Sorry!" gasped Abigail. "I didn't mean . . . You startled me! Did you really speak?"

"Humans!" said the rat. "Can't trust their own senses! You won't catch rats being so stupid. Believe what you bite, I always say. And pick up that grape, will you? You made me drop it and I hadn't finished. Wipe it first!" she added sharply.

Abigail obediently picked up the grape, wiped it and handed it back to the rat. Gnasher sat up on her shoulder and held the grape in her front paws, nibbling elegantly.

"Why did you never talk before?" asked Abigail. She felt better now that she had got over her surprise. Apart from talking, Gnasher was acting like a rat, doing what she always did.

"You never asked," said Gnasher.

"You really will help me be a witch, then?"

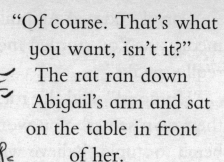

"Of course. That's what you want, isn't it?" The rat ran down Abigail's arm and sat on the table in front of her.

"Yes!" agreed Abigail. Her eyes shone. "Oh, yes!"

"First things first," said Gnasher. She curled her tail over her back, gave her whiskers a quick wipe and peered at Abigail out of bright black eyes. "There's a catch to doing magic. Two, really. First, you must be sure of what you want to do. It's no use starting something and then whining, 'Oh, dear. I didn't mean to do that!' What do you *really* want?"

Abigail didn't hesitate. "I want to get back at Ryan!"

"Right!" said the rat. "He deserves anything he gets. But before we start,

24

there's another catch, remember?"

Abigail was impatient. "Well?"

"You can't ever tell a lie. And I mean that. *You won't be able to*. Think you can live with that?"

Abigail didn't hesitate. "I'm a rotten liar anyway," she said. "That's OK!"

"Hmm," said Gnasher. "Maybe. Just remember, it isn't always easy! It can get you into trouble." She combed her whiskers again. "Now, we need a Plan. What, exactly, do you want to do to him?"

"I want to turn him into a frog!" said Abigail. "Listen, this is the spell I made up today – *'Ryan James ought to be a frog'*–"

"No, no!" Gnasher stopped her. "You'll have to do better than that. Just saying he ought to be a frog won't do at all. Umm. What rhymes with . . . ? Never mind, there's no hurry, we've got all weekend."

It took all Saturday morning but at last they had a spell.

"I suppose," said Abigail, "we ought to test it. As it's our first."

"Try it on your mum," suggested Gnasher.

"*No!*" yelled Abigail.

"All right, all right! Just asking. You think of something, then."

"How about testing it on you?" Abigail asked.

"Absolutely *not!*"

"Could we try turning a toad into a frog?"

"Well! A sensible idea at last!" Gnasher climbed into Abigail's pocket. "The boating pond will be the best place to find a toad."

They found a large fat toad under a bush near the boating pond in the park. It looked contented. It blinked its golden eyes at Abigail and didn't bother to move.

"Hadn't we better ask if it wants to be a frog?" whispered Abigail. The toad did look so peaceful, squatting on the damp earth. It seemed rude to disturb it.

"Why? It's just a matter of turning one sort of amphibian into another," Gnasher muttered back.

"Couldn't you ask it?"

"You're the one who suddenly has cold feet," said Gnasher unkindly. "You ask it."

"But it won't understand me!"

The rat sighed. "You're a witch now, Abigail. If you really want that toad to understand you, it will."

Abigail crouched down. "Er, excuse me, Mr Toad. Would you mind if I tried to turn you into a frog? Just for practice."

The toad blinked again. "Frog?" he said in a creaky voice. "One of those noisy, bouncing cousins of mine? Hmmm. What's in it for me, huh?"

Abigail didn't know what to say.

Gnasher did. "You'll be much faster," she pointed out. "Catch more flies, have more fun."

"OK," said the toad. "Go ahead."

Abigail still felt uncomfortable about it. "Er, I need to know your name," she told him. "I have to put it in the spell, instead of Ryan's."

The toad grinned at her. "Cree-akk'gh," he said.

Abigail stared. "That's your name?"

"Correct," said the toad.

Abigail practised it several times. She felt uneasy. It really didn't seem right to do this. But she carefully said the spell they'd worked out. Then she held her breath until she had to let it out.

Nothing happened.

The toad shrugged, snapped at a small fly, missed and began to shuffle away. "That's life," he remarked. "You win some, you lose some. See you around, kid."

"Goodbye, Cree-akk," said Abigail in a small voice.

"Cree-akk'gh," corrected the toad. He waddled under a low branch and vanished among the dead leaves.

"It *was* a spell meant to turn a human

into a frog," Gnasher said. She ran up Abigail's arm and rubbed herself against Abigail's neck. "Cheer up! I'm sure it will work when you really want it to. On Ryan!"

Chapter Five

A Rat in the Classroom

On Monday Abigail took Gnasher to
school in her pocket. The rat had
promised to keep as quiet and still as
possible. Of course, if Abigail cast a spell,
Gnasher would have to move to help
her. And this time it would work. She
was sure of it. Well, almost sure. Fairly
sure.

She shivered with excitement. Look
out, Ryan James! One wrong word and
– *ribbit! ribbit!*

But once in the classroom, Gnasher
did not keep still. She heaved herself
round and round in Abigail's pocket
until she'd wriggled her pointy nose out.
Her whiskers twitched and her nose
wrinkled. She even squeaked, very softly.

Abigail bent down as if she wanted to tie her shoelace. "What on earth is the matter?" she breathed. "Do keep still, Gnasher."

Gnasher reached up as far as she could. Her whiskers tickled Abigail's ear. 'There's a witch in this classroom!' she whispered.

Abigail blinked. "Of course there is! Me."

"Not you, stupid. Someone else. I can smell it!"

"Abigail!" said Mrs Treasure. "Please sit down. This is a maths lesson, not gymnastics."

Abigail hastily sat down, very red in the face. She did try to pay attention to the lesson, but it wasn't easy. All sorts of questions kept jumping into her mind. "Who is this other witch? Could it be Pat? No, can't see Pat with a Familiar. Tara? Too giggly. I'm sure witches don't giggle all the time. Sophie? She's nasty enough! Oh, I do hope it isn't Sophie. Can whoever it is smell me out? Can I believe Gnasher? She seemed certain but . . ."

Abigail dragged her mind back. Mrs Treasure was getting cross. Not with her, luckily. With Sophie.

Sophie never paid attention in maths. Today, she twisted herself round and made faces at anyone who'd look.

"Sophie!" said Mrs Treasure, "Turn round."

Sophie took no notice. But somehow nobody would look at her any more. Making faces was no fun. Sophie turned back.

Mrs Treasure was staring silently at her. She was really angry. Even Sophie could see that. For once, Sophie didn't look innocent or mocking. She looked scared. She ducked her head. "Sorry, miss," she muttered.

Abigail blinked. She watched Sophie take out her workbook and pen as meekly as if she had never answered a teacher back in her life.

Abigail began to wonder if perhaps today was the right day to start on her career as a witch.

She dithered until first play. Then Ryan bumped against her in the cloakroom and felt the soft lump that was Gnasher in her pocket. "Hey, whatcher got?" he said.

Abigail twisted away. "Nothing to do with you, nosy," she snapped.

Ryan stuck his hand into her pocket. He dragged Gnasher out by the tail. Gnasher twisted round and bit him. Ryan yelped and jumped back. He flung the rat away.

"Gnasher!" screamed Abigail. She leapt. She stretched frantically. Her fingertips just reached the falling rat. Gnasher rolled into her hands.

For a moment Abigail cuddled the trembling rat. Then Ryan reached for her. Abigail glared at him. Her hands were full, so she kicked his ankle. Ryan yelled in pain and rage. He hopped, wobbled, and sat down. Hard.

"Now, Abigail! Now!" squealed Gnasher.

"You're a frog, Ryan James, you're a frog,"

began Abigail. She gabbled out the words of the spell as fast as she could:

"Slimy and jumpy, bug-eyed and lumpy,
Ryan James, Ryan James, you're a frog,

Like a bump on a log in a bog,
You're a frog, Ryan James, you're a
*   frog!"*

This time she meant it with all her
heart.

Chapter Six

A Frog in the Cloakroom

Abigail stared at the small greeny-brown frog on the hard stone floor. It panted. Its golden eyes bulged. It looked absolutely terrified.

"Oh, poor thing!" Abigail crouched down and reached to pick it up. It wobbled, tried to jump away and fell over.

"Not much good at being a frog, is he?" said Gnasher. She climbed down Abigail's skirt and ran over to the frog. "Get up on her hand, wart-face!" she told it. "Do you want to be squashed when everyone comes back in? Go on, hop to it!"

The frog gasped and flattened itself on the floor. Gnasher chittered her teeth at it. With a huge effort, the frog scrambled up onto Abigail's hand. The rat followed. She walked calmly over the cowering frog and ran up to Abigail's shoulder. She tucked herself behind Abigail's hair. "Now what?" she asked.

Abigail hadn't thought past turning Ryan into a frog. To tell the truth, after their failure with the toad, she'd only thought of making the spell work. Now it had and Abigail had no idea what to do next. "Umm," she said. "Turn him back?"

"Just like a human!" said Gnasher.

"Go to all this trouble and then it's 'Turn him back.' Do you even know how?" The rat sniffed. "No, you don't. And don't look at me! I'm not the witch around here. I'm just the Familiar."

"But what can I do?" wailed Abigail.

"Kiss him?"

"Yeucch!" Abigail shuddered. "Anyway, I'm not a princess."

"Drop him in the wildlife pond, then, and forget him." Gnasher cleaned busily behind her ears.

"I can't do that!" Abigail felt like crying. "I can't leave him like this! Whatever will his mum and dad do?"

"You should have thought of that before," the rat told her.

Abigail stared at the frog. The frog stared back. Its throat went in and out, in and out.

"Can you speak?" Abigail asked it at last.

"Your hands are too hot," complained the frog.

It sounded just like Ryan in his whiney mood. Abigail felt a bit more comfortable about the whole affair.

"OK," she said. "I'll put you in the pocket of my jacket. Hang on, I'll wet my hanky first and wrap you in it."

The frog looked disgusted. It had the right sort of face for it. "That hanky is filthy," it said. "I want a clean one."

Gnasher walked down Abigail's arm. She showed the frog all her sharp yellow teeth. "Then Want must be your master, ducky," she said. "Or would you rather be dropped down the nearest drain?"

The frog swelled its throat sulkily but said no more. Abigail wrapped it carefully in her wet hanky and tucked it into the left-hand pocket of her jacket. She hung up the jacket on her peg.

"You'll have to stay here for a bit," she said. "Don't wander off, will you? I'll try to find out how to turn you back as soon as I can," she promised, patting the moist lump gently.

But she had no idea where to start.

Chapter Seven

A Witch in the Garden

Abigail soon realized that she couldn't even try to help Ryan until dinner time.

There was a tremendous fuss when Mrs Treasure saw that Ryan was missing. Everyone was asked where they'd last seen him.

Abigail told the exact truth. "I saw him in the cloakroom," she said, "just before the bell went. He was still there when I left."

Mrs Treasure fetched the Head. The Head asked them all the same questions Mrs Treasure had already asked. He looked very stern. "We must let his mother know," he said to Mrs Treasure.

"She's at work," said Mrs Treasure.

"Then she'll have to leave work,"

snapped the Head. "Or do you think we should notify the police first?"

The teachers were so worried that they didn't try to keep their voices down. The whole class listened eagerly and itched with excitement.

Nobody did much work after that. The people near the window bobbed up and down, telling the others what was happening in the playground. Mrs Treasure had to keep telling them to sit down.

"The Head's out there now!"

"The caretaker's searching the wildlife garden!"

"They're going to drag the pond!"

"Nah, it's only knee deep. They'll just prod it a bit."

"They're looking in the outside toilets!" reported Tara, giggling. "I wouldn't hide there. Yuck!"

"He's run away. He's scared of Mrs Treasure!" sniggered Michael.

Abigail kept quiet.

Ryan's mum came. She was big and cross. And loud. She shouted at Mrs Treasure. She was rude to the Head and really horrible to the school secretary. Mrs Treasure did not tell her that Abigail was the last person to have seen Ryan. Abigail was very relieved. She had taken a strong dislike to Ryan's mum.

As soon as they were let out for dinner play, Abigail fled to the cloakroom. She lifted her jacket gently from its peg and put her hand into the pocket on the left.

There was the wet hanky. But . . .

"Where's Ryan?" gasped Abigail.

start here

She fumbled hastily in the right-hand pocket. No frog. She crouched down to peer under coats and between shoes. Still no frog.

"The others will be here in a moment! Gnasher, what can we do?" she demanded.

"Ryan, you idiot!" Gnasher squeaked loudly. "Come on out. It's us!"

Nothing happened.

Abigail felt desperate. "I told him to stay put!" she wailed. "Isn't this just like him? Of all the stupid, idiotic, pig-headed donkeys, he's the worst!"

"Stop mewling and put me down," said Gnasher. "Perhaps I can sniff his trail."

She ran to and fro across the floor. Abigail hopped up and down by the door, ready to warn the rat if anyone came. Then Gnasher stiffened. "Got him!" she said. "He went outside!"

Abigail dragged her jacket on,

scooped up her Familiar and hurried out into the playground. "Which way?" she asked.

"How should I know?" Gnasher was annoyed. "You know I can't see far. Where would you go if you were a frog?"

"But I'd be an Abigail frog, not a Ryan frog. I wouldn't do the same thing!"

Gnasher squeaked in rage.

"All right, all right," Abigail said hastily. "I think I'd make for the wildlife garden. It's only a little way. A frog could hide in the plants, so he'd feel safe . . . and there's the pond if he got too dry. They've looked there once, so they won't go there again and maybe tread on him."

It seemed the only possible place. Abigail slipped along by the fence and peered all around. No-one was looking. She crouched down and scuttled through the gate into the garden.

"Whew! Safe!" She scrunched herself up small behind a bush. "Can you smell him, Gnasher?"

Gnasher's nose wiggled. Her whiskers twitched. "Yes! There he is, the mushy pea-brain!"

She made a sudden rush into the grass. A frog shot out. It landed near Abigail but, before she could catch it, it gave a huge graceful leap and splashed down in the pond.

Abigail scrambled over and crouched down to peer into the dark water. The frog had completely vanished. A damp, rotting-leaf smell drifted up.

"Are you sure that was the right frog?" Abigail asked.

Gnasher came and looked into the pond. "Of course I'm sure! He must think he really is a frog. Well, didn't you tell me that he's the best swimmer in your year? So leave him to it. He'll be all right."

"No! How can I? Everyone knows I was the last person to see him. I've got to find him and turn him back. That awful mum of his is bound to ask questions. She scares me! I can't say I turned him into a frog. They'll put me in the loony bin!"

"I warned you, right at the start," said the rat.

"And," wailed Abigail, "I can't even lie about it!"

"Told you so," said Gnasher.

Abigail was cold and frightened. The leaves and grass were damp and it had begun to rain. She was getting more uncomfortable by the minute. She lost her temper. "You – you rat, Gnasher!" she snarled. "Just get lost!"

The rat vanished.

"Oh, no!" Abigail stared around her. "Gnasher? Gnasher! Come back! I didn't mean it. Oh, what shall I do?"

Chapter Eight

A Lizard in the Plot

A greyish lizard strolled out of the grass. It walked right up to Abigail and poked its snout at her hand. "I thought so!" it said.

Abigail scrambled to her feet. "Who are you?" she asked. Her voice shook a little. "What do you want?"

The lizard peered up at Abigail with one bright eye. "I am the Familiar of the witch in residence at this school," it announced. "As such, it is my duty to look into all cases of unauthorized spelling committed on these premises." It flicked its long slim tail and cocked its head to look at Abigail from the other eye.

"If you're a Familiar, whose are you?

And what's your name?" she demanded.

"You may address me as Somerset," said the lizard grandly. "And the frog that just now escaped you, is, I imagine, the missing Ryan?"

Abigail nodded. "It was me who turned him into a frog," she confessed. "I'm a witch."

"Of course you are," said the lizard calmly. "But you're not a very good one. You couldn't even change him back into a human, could you?"

Abigail stared miserably at the pond. "No, I don't know how," she said. "And now I've lost him – and Gnasher too.

Oh, wherever has she gone?"

"Never lose your temper with your Familiar," said the lizard. "But don't worry, she'll find her way back, sometime."

"Sometime!" said Abigail, in horror.

"Your main problem is Ryan. If you don't get him back to normal soon," said the lizard, "there'll be real trouble. Any minute now, they'll be calling the police in."

"Oh, stop it, please!" begged Abigail. "I never meant— Oh! That's what Gnasher said, right at the beginning. She said it would be no use saying that I didn't mean to do something . . . Oh, please, Somerset, help me!"

"Of course," said Somerset smugly. "My witch sent me to do just that."

Abigail was so indignant that she couldn't speak. Who does this witch think she is? she thought. Sending a snooty lizard to do – well, what I can't do! It was quite true. She *did* need his help. "How do we get Ryan to come out?" she asked.

Somerset looked into the water. "We could just transform all the frogs into people and see which one turns out to be Ryan," he suggested casually.

Abigail imagined dozens of strange boys – and girls, of course – suddenly standing around, dripping, not knowing how to be people. They'd try to jump and catch flies!

"No!" she cried. "It'd be awful!"

"I think it'd be fun," said the lizard. "Come on, let's do it!"

"No." Abigail was very firm. "No, we must find Ryan."

"Mind you, it's probably done him a world of good," said Somerset. "Still, you're right. A Summoning, then." His tail lashed suddenly. His beady eyes shone. He was almost hopping with excitement.

"A what?" Abigail blinked at him.

"A Calling. You call someone to you," explained the lizard, "using a drop of your blood and something that belongs to him. A hair or a nail clipping is best. Or his blood, of course."

"Ugh!" Abigail didn't fancy that at all. "I haven't got anything of Ryans's," she pointed out.

"Yes, you have. That hanky you wrapped him in. It's still wet, isn't it? It should have a tiny bit of him stuck to it."

Abigail pulled out the crumpled hanky and spread it out. She peered at it. Was that a minute piece of skin? She hoped the lizard was right.

"How do I get a drop of blood?" she asked unwillingly.

"Quick! Get down! There's someone coming," Somerset hissed.

Abigail crouched down hastily. Stupid to have forgotten she could be seen! "Ouch!" There were long thorns on the bush next to her.

"There you go," said the lizard cheerfully. "Blood!"

Abigail held up a scratched hand. Two large drops of blood welled up. "You did that on purpose!" she accused.

The lizard wriggled happily. "Don't waste it," he said. "Catch it on the hanky. And don't stand up," he added.

"There really is someone looking this way."

Abigail felt very glad that her jacket was a boring brown colour. She was well hidden among the autumn leaves. She blotted her scratch on the damp hanky. "Now what?"

"Call him. By the Power of Blood. Go on, say it!"

Abigail hesitated. Somehow she didn't like calling Ryan with her own blood. But she could hear distant shouts of "Ryan! Where are you, lad?" from across the playground and up and down the road. She had to do it.

"Ryan James, I call you by the Power of Blood. Come out! Come now!" It sounded rather good, she thought.

There was a plop. A frog had hopped out of the pond and was staring at them. Its throat went in and out rapidly. It looked ready to leap back any second.

"What do I do now?" whispered Abigail. "I ought to have practised!"

"Just point and tell him to be in his true shape," Somerset told her.

"That's all?" Abigail couldn't believe it.

"That's all." Somerset sounded impatient. "Get on!"

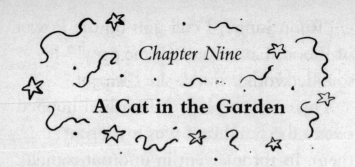

Chapter Nine

A Cat in the Garden

Abigail swallowed and took a deep breath. She pointed. "Be in your true shape!" she told the frog.

The frog twitched violently. "Ribbit," it said. "Ribbit."

"Nothing's happened!" Abigail was shocked. "You said just to tell him! You said it would work! Why hasn't it worked? What's gone wrong?"

"You didn't say his name," said the lizard. "Surely even you know enough to do that! Ignorant human!" he added scornfully.

"You never said that!" shouted Abigail. She forgot to hide, she forgot Ryan, she forgot everything except that hateful lizard. "How do I know it's not a

real frog? Suppose I said to you,
'Somerset, be in your true shape,'
nothing would . . . uh . . . happen . . ."
Her voice trailed off. She lowered her
pointing finger. Her mouth fell open.

The lizard was writhing. He stretched.
He grew slowly larger.

Abigail clapped a hand over her
mouth. Her eyes opened wider and
wider. What have I done? she thought,
horrified. Had she somehow damaged
the lizard? The lizard's shape was
blurring now, faster and faster. Abigail
blinked and had to look away. It made
her dizzy to watch.

When she looked back, she stood frozen in astonishment.

"Why don't you shut your mouth?" suggested the big grey cat at her feet. "You look remarkably silly, even for a human." He began to wash himself furiously.

Abigail shook her head. She rubbed her eyes. The cat was still there.

He was a handsome cat, dark blue-grey with a neat white shirt front and white paws. He gave her a long stare from brilliant green eyes, then turned to wash a back paw, spitting out bits of mud with a disgusted expression.

"You're not really a lizard!" Abigail felt dazed. "You weren't in your true shape!"

The cat looked her over.
"Marvellous!" he said. "Really, really, observant. No, I am not a lizard. I am a cat. C-A-T. Cat. Any more blinding glimpses of the obvious?" He held his tail

down with a paw and washed the tip.

"But – but –" Abigail stuttered, "you are Somerset, aren't you? You are still a Familiar?"

"Right." Somerset began on his tummy.

Abigail cleared her throat. "Do – um – do you like being a Familiar?" she asked.

Somerset looked surprised. "Cats only do what they want to," he pointed out. "Of course I like it. Magic! It smells of wonder. It's exciting. It's like electricity running through you."

I suppose that's why Gnasher wanted to be my Familiar, thought Abigail. Oh! She almost spoke aloud in her excitement. I wonder! Can I trick Somerset into telling who the other witch is?

"Somerset," she said carefully, "why

were you a lizard? Why would anyone want to turn a handsome cat like you into a lizard?"

"Some people," said the cat, "are never satisfied. She said my beautiful fur made her sneeze! So she turned me into a lizard. *Me!* Pah! It would have served her right if I'd been the fire-breathing sort and burnt her up!"

"That's awful!" Abigail glanced nervously over her shoulder. She felt that talking about her might make the other witch appear.

"Enough gossip," said Somerset briskly. He padded over to the pond. The frog was still crouched on the edge. It hadn't moved.

"Oh, dooms! I forgot all about him!" Abigail was shocked at herself. She crawled after the cat and sat back on her heels to stare at the frog. "It must be Ryan, mustn't it? I mean, he was Called. And he hasn't moved an inch."

"He can't, until he's dismissed," explained Somerset. "Try again."

Abigail hesitated. "Ryan?" she said gently. "It's all right. You'll change back this time."

"No!" said the frog. "Don't want to. Shan't. You can't make me! Nor my mum can't, neither."

"But you can't stay a frog for ever!" Abigail looked at Somerset. "He can't, can he?"

"Oh, yes. It doesn't happen often," said the cat, "but some folk do prefer the simple life."

"But . . ." Abigail didn't know what to say. Ryan must have a pretty miserable time with that terrifying mum. She could see that he might like being a carefree frog. "But what about me? And the school? We'll all be in dreadful trouble if you don't turn up soon!"

"Why should I care? They'll never find me," said the frog smugly.

"Mmmm." Somerset stretched out a paw and tapped the frog, very gently. "You know, Ryan, there's more to being a frog than just hopping around or swimming. There are cats that enjoy playing with frogs. Catch it, let it go, let it jump, grab it out of the air . . . Great fun! Then there are herons. They just love a nice juicy frog for tea. Let him go, Abigail. He'll be fun to catch again." He stretched his paw so that all the claws shot out like knives.

"No!" croaked the frog. "All right, all right, change me back."

Abigail pointed her finger. "Ryan James, be in your true shape!"

This time, it worked.

Unfortunately, no-one had thought how close Ryan was to the water.

Chapter Ten

A Boy in the Water

Ryan teetered on his heels for a moment, yelling and waving his arms. Abigail jumped up and grabbed him.

Too late.

Splosh! Ryan went over backwards, full length into the pond. Abigail wiped smelly pond water from her eyes in time to see Somerset, spitting furiously, streak into the bushes.

The smell of rotting leaves was overpowering. Ryan's fall had thoroughly stirred up the bottom of the pond. Abigail coughed, held her breath and reached for Ryan's hand. He sat up but didn't seem able to get any further.

"Come on, Ryan, you can't stay there!"

Ryan just stared at her. Abigail wondered if she ought to step into the pond and haul him up but the smell was too much for her. And she was quite wet enough already.

"Get up, you idiot!" she snapped.

Slowly, Ryan climbed to his feet. Abigail reached out again and pulled him to land. Ryan dragged himself out of the water and stood dripping on the bank. He was pale, trembling and tearful and soaking wet.

"Where am I?" he said. "Why am I

all wet?" Then he bent over and was sick on the ground. And again. And again.

"I'd better take you to the sickroom," said Abigail anxiously.

But she didn't have to.

"Well done, Abigail!" exclaimed Mrs Treasure from the garden gate. "You clever girl, you found him." She hurried over to them and took Ryan's hand. "Come along, Ryan, we'll soon have you warm and dry again. Come on, Abigail."

Ryan was swept away to be stripped, washed, rubbed down and rolled in blankets. The school secretary phoned for an ambulance. Mrs Treasure tried to make Ryan's mum stop shouting at him.

Abigail washed the mud from her hands and knees and the pond water from her face.

When she was dry, she went to the Head's office. The Head wanted to talk to her. Mrs Treasure wanted to talk to her. Abigail could hear Ryan's mum in the corridor. She was shouting that she was going to sue the school. *She* wanted a word with Abigail, too.

Abigail was glad when the door was shut. She felt sorry for the school secretary but thankful that no-one wanted to let Mrs James in.

"Now, Abigail, how did you come to find Ryan?" asked the Head.

"I thought where I'd be if I was Ryan," Abigail explained, "and I went there and he was."

Mrs Treasure smiled. The Head frowned. "You just walked into the garden and there he was? Why did he fall in the pond?"

"He was right on the edge of it." Abigail shrugged. "Perhaps he was startled."

"Did you know that he doesn't remember anything after going to the cloakroom at first play?" asked the Head.

Abigail gave a silent sigh of relief. "Really?" she said. "He really can't remember? He did say 'Where am I?' when I pulled him out. And he didn't know how he'd got wet."

"Shock," said the Head. "The boy had some sort of shock."

"I think, Headmaster, that I should take Abigail back to the dining room, now," said Mrs Treasure. "She's had no dinner yet. She must be hungry."

There was no noise from the corridor. Mrs James had left in the ambulance that had taken Ryan to hospital.

"For a check-up," said Mrs Treasure cheerfully. "But I'm sure he'll be fine. Probably back at school tomorrow!"

Chapter Eleven

A Witch in the Bedroom

Abigail hoped Ryan wouldn't come back for a long time. Suppose he got his memory back? Or had only been pretending all along? Would he tell people that she'd turned him into a frog?

His mum doesn't look like the sort to listen much, she thought hopefully. I bet she never pays any attention unless he gets into real trouble. And then I bet she just bashes him. Poor Ryan. Glad I'm not him. She was surprised at herself. She never thought she'd feel sorry for Ryan!

What would happen when Ryan came back? And who was the other witch? But, most important of all, *where was Gnasher*? And would she ever come back?

Abigail ran all the way home after school, hoping desperately that she'd find Gnasher safely in her cage.

The cage was empty.

Abigail sat down beside it and burst into tears. "It's the worst day of my life!" she sobbed. "Oh, Gnasher, my poor Gnasher! Where are you? I wish you were here!" And she cried till her nose was bunged up and her eyes were sore.

At last she stopped crying and began to think. Gnasher had been magicked away. Perhaps magic could bring her back?

"What about that Summoning spell!" she said aloud. "I've got lots of bits of Gnasher in her bed, hairs and stuff. What a good thing I haven't changed her litter yet! And the scratch on my hand – I can pick off the scab and get some more blood, no problem. But will it work without a Familiar? Somerset was helping me before. But what else can I do? I'll have to try."

Abigail dripped several drops of blood onto Gnasher's bed and Called. "Gnasher Rat, by the Power of my blood, I call you home. Come to me, my Familiar, come home! Please, Gnasher!" she added. The rat hated to be given orders.

She waited, listening hard. Nothing.

She rested her forehead on the table, shut her eyes and Willed Gnasher to come home. Her head began to spin. Her ears rang. She felt as if she would burst. She Willed harder.

There was a soft thump on the table beside her and a cross chittering noise.

"Gnasher!" yelled Abigail.

She was muddy and had a nasty scratch on her tail. Her fur was bedraggled and her whiskers askew. But Gnasher was safely home.

And she was in a very bad temper.

Abigail fetched a damp soft cloth and gently wiped away the mud. She boiled some peas in milk for Gnasher's favourite meal and sprinkled fresh coriander over them. She picked out sunflower seeds and pumpkin seeds and fed them to the rat one by one. She got a slice of Stilton cheese from the kitchen, when Mum wasn't looking, and crumbled it over a lettuce leaf.

Gnasher ate until her tummy bulged. Then she washed her face, combed her whiskers and wanted to know what had happened to Ryan. "And how did you know how to Call me?" she asked. "I never taught you that spell."

So Abigail told her about the lizard. "His name's Somerset and he's the other witch's Familiar," she explained. "But—"

"Somerset?" Gnasher sniggered. "What a name for a lizard!"

"But he's a cat, really," Abigail told her. "I think it's quite a good name for a cat."

Gnasher froze. "A cat?" She bristled her fur. "You were hobnobbing with a *cat*?"

"He helped me a lot! I could never have got Ryan back to normal – well, almost normal – without him," Abigail protested. She told Gnasher the rest of the story.

"And you still don't know who the

other witch is?" Gnasher climbed into her cage. "Well, I'm bushed. I'm going to sleep now. We'll have to see about her in the morning. Don't wake me up when you come to bed!"

Chapter Twelve

A Spell in the Classroom

The next morning Abigail was still
worried about the other witch. Gnasher
didn't want to get up but Abigail
grabbed the rat from her cage and
stuffed her into her pocket.

The rat was not pleased.

"You must help me find the other witch!" Abigail begged. "Please!"

"Huh!" said Gnasher. "Oh, very well. I suppose we do need to know."

It was a lovely day. The wind had blown all the rain away in the night. The bright sun and the warm air made Abigail feel cheerful. She hung up her jacket in the cloakroom, humming happily.

Full of hope, she went along to the classroom. And stopped in the doorway.

Ryan was back!

Abigail bit her lip. She went silently to her chair. Ryan was sitting next to her as usual. He was looking pale and sorry for himself. Abigail waited for him to speak. But he didn't. He never said a word about what had happened to him yesterday.

It was very strange. Ryan really didn't seem to remember being a frog at all! Abigail sighed with relief and relaxed.

When people asked Ryan why he'd disappeared, he mumbled something about being ill.

"Something he ate, perhaps," Abigail told everyone. "He was sick three times!"

People gazed respectfully at Ryan's pasty face. Pat gave him a barley sugar to suck. Even Sophie didn't laugh at him.

"Do you suppose the other witch made him forget, somehow?" Abigail asked Gnasher at play time. She was glad she'd got the rat with her. Gnasher made a comforting warmth in her pocket.

The rat wiggled her whiskers. "Don't know," she said. "Maybe people never do remember being changed. Perhaps it's just too much for them."

"Oh, poor Ryan!" said Abigail.

"You're getting soft. Going to be nice to him?" asked Gnasher.

Abigail stuck out her chin. "Maybe. If he doesn't start jabbing his pencil into me again."

Ryan was very quiet all day and never once stuck his pencil into Abigail or anyone else. He didn't even sharpen it as he usually did. Abigail caught him staring at her once but he didn't say anything.

Mrs Treasure was different today. She'd had her hair cut short and she was wearing a smart suit in deep red. No-one had ever seen her in anything but porridgey colours.

She behaved differently, too. She was deaf to George's whines, she ticked off several people for talking and Tara for giggling. Everyone was amazed.

Sophie was the only one who didn't take warning. She was worse than usual. She wriggled and chatted all the time Mrs Treasure was telling them what they were to do, she made faces at the giggliest girls and,

at last, she tipped back her chair until she tipped it right over onto Pat and Michael. The back of Sophie's head bashed Michael's nose. It began to bleed. Michael yelled with pain. Sophie laughed.

Pat didn't yell. She got up, hauled Sophie to her feet and made to belt her one.

"Thank you, Pat," said Mrs Treasure firmly. "I shall deal with Sophie. Take Michael to the sickroom for me, will you? I'll be with you very shortly."

When Pat and Michael had gone, Mrs Treasure made Sophie stand in front of the class. "I know we had a great deal of excitement yesterday," she told the class. "I know that it is hard for you to settle down and work today. I am sorry that Sophie is making it so difficult for you. But Sophie's silliness will stop if you all ignore her. Pay no attention to her.

Pretend she isn't here.
I shall do the same."

She turned to Sophie. "Sophie
Jackson," she said in a slow, calm voice,
"from this moment on, nobody in this
class will see or hear you while you are
behaving badly."

Abigail stiffened all over. She felt
Gnasher give a great leap in her pocket.
The magic power behind Mrs Treasure's
words was like an electric shock.

"Gnasher!" whispered Abigail. "It's her! It's Mrs Treasure! *She's* the witch in the classroom!"

They stared and shivered together.

"I'm scared," Abigail told Gnasher. "Do you think she'll do something to us? Now she knows I'm a witch?"

"She must have known all along. She sent Somerset to help you, didn't she? Why should she harm you  now?" Gnasher snapped.

"Well, I did turn her Familiar back into a cat," Abigail reminded her.

"But," said Gnasher, "does she know that?"

The afternoon dragged on. At last, it was going home time. Mrs Treasure beckoned to Abigail.

Abigail waited for the room to empty.

She felt cold.

"Abigail, dear," said Mrs Treasure, "do you know where my Familiar, Somerset, is? I haven't seen him since I sent him to help you yesterday. Yet when I spelled Sophie, I felt him helping me. He must be here somewhere!"

Abigail opened her mouth. But before she could speak, Somerset strolled into the room, purring loudly. He rubbed against Abigail's legs.

Mrs Treasure stared at him in horror.

"Somerset! You're a cat again! A-a-a-tchoo!" She grabbed for a hanky.

"I'm sorry," said Abigail. "I unspelled him by accident."

Mrs Treasure shook her head and blew her nose. "Some accidents are more accidental than others. I suspect Somerset arranged this one. Did you mind being a lizard so much, Somerset?"

"Yes, I did!" said Somerset. "I hated it. But don't worry. I intend to go and live with Abigail and be her Familiar. *She* won't mess me around!"

"But," Abigail began, "what about Gnasher?"

"That's all right," said Somerset. "She can still be your Familiar. Junior to me, of course."

"Cheek!" Gnasher scrambled out of Abigail's pocket, fairly chittering with rage.

"You've only just started, rat, and I've been at this for a long time," Somerset smirked. He licked a paw. The claws showed, just a little.

"You leave Gnasher alone!" Abigail put her hand over the rat. "She's my best friend. If you want to be my Familiar, you'll have to be nice to her. Polite. No claws! All right?" She was surprised at how fierce she sounded.

"No problem," said Somerset. "As if any Familiar would ever harm another Familiar! Right, Gnasher?"

"Right," said Gnasher, showing her sharp teeth. "No problem. None at all!"

Somerset winked and rubbed against Abigail again. "See you later," he said – and vanished.

Mrs Treasure sneezed again violently and wiped her nose. Her eyes were watering. "It's no good," she said sadly. "I just can't be anywhere near a cat. A-a-a-tschoo!"

"You could try another Familiar,"
suggested Abigail.

Mrs Treasure sighed. "It's not that
easy," she said. "You have to find one
who actually enjoys magic. There aren't
many around."

"I know a toad who might like it,"
Abigail told her. "His name's Cree-
akk'gh. He lives in the park. I'll
introduce you if you want."

"That's very thoughtful of you,

Abigail. I appreciate it." Mrs Treasure patted her shoulder. "After school tomorrow? But I do think, Abigail, that you'd better keep your magic out of school in future, don't you? We can't have two witches in the classroom!"

"Of course," Abigail agreed. She smiled at Mrs Treasure. "One witch in the classroom is enough."

THE END

BLACK QUEEN
Michael Morpurgo

My blood ran cold. The Black Queen was looking down at me from out of the sun.

The 'Black Queen' is what Billy calls his shadowy next-door neighbour. She always wears a black cloak and a wide-brimmed black hat. She lurks about her garden, alone except for her black cat. Scarily for Billy, the Black Queen befriends him and asks him to look after her cat while she's away. Billy can't resist the opportunity to peek inside her house. There are chessboards scattered everywhere. Who is the Black Queen and what sort of game is she playing? Billy thinks he knows . . .

A brilliantly intriguing novel for younger readers from the award-winning author of *The Butterfly Lion* and *The Wreck of the Zanzibar*.

0 552 546453

YOUNG CORGI
Books to get your teeth into!

LIZZIE ZIPMOUTH
Jacqueline Wilson

'**Why** don't you ever say anything, Lizzie?'
said Rory. 'It's like you've got a zip
across your mouth.'

Lizzie has zipped up her mouth. She
doesn't want to talk to Rory or Jake, her
new stepbrothers, or Sam, their dad, or
even her mum. She's totally fed up at
having to join a new family and nothing
can coax her into speaking to them. Not
football, not pizza, not a new bedroom.
That is, until she meets a member of
the new family who is even more
stubborn than her – and has had
a lot more practice!

A funny, touching story from the best-
selling author of *The Suitcase Kid*, *Bad
Girls* and *Double Act*. An ideal book for
younger readers, perfect for building
reading confidence.

0 552 546534

YOUNG CORGI
Books to get your teeth into!

All Transworld titles are available by post from:

Bookpost, PO Box 29, Douglas, Isle of Man, IM99 1BQ

Credit cards accepted. Please telephone 01624 836000,
fax 01624 837033, Internet http://www.bookpost.co.uk
or e-mail: bookshop@enterprise.net for details

Free postage and packing in the UK. Overseas customers:
allow £1 per book (paperbacks) and £3 per book (hardbacks)